First Experiences

GOING TO A PARTY

Anne Civardi
Illustrated by Stephen Cartwright

Reading Consultant: Betty Ro___

There is a little yellow duck hiding on every two pages. Can you find it?

The Dunns

MERRY

DAD DUNN

MUM DUNN

NELLIE DUNN

NED DUNN

HARVEY

This is the Dunn family. Nellie is five and Ned is three.
Ned has a puppy called Harvey.

The Invitation

PETE

Pete, the postman, gives Nellie a big letter. It is an invitation to Larry Lamb's party on Saturday.

Making Monster Costumes

Larry is having a fancy dress party. He wants all his friends to come dressed up as fierce monsters.

Granny Dunn helps Mum and Dad make two monster costumes. But Grandpa is being a bit of a nuisance.

Choosing a Present

Mum takes Nellie and Ned to the toyshop to choose a present for Larry. Nellie wants to buy him this robot.

Ready to Go

On Saturday Ned and Nellie get dressed in their costumes. They are ready to go to the party.

The Monster Party

Nellie gives Larry his present. He is six years old today.
Ned thinks it is fun to frighten the cat.

Lots of other monsters have already arrived. They all try to guess who is wearing each mask.

Opening the Presents

All Larry's friends have brought him a present. He is very pleased with the robot from Nellie and Ned.

Mum Lamb writes a list of who gave him each present.
He has lots of thank-you letters to write tomorrow.

The Birthday Tea

At last it is time for tea. Mum and Granny Lamb have made all sorts of delicious things to eat.

Larry has a chocolate birthday cake with a ghost on the top. Can he blow out all his candles at once?

Party Games

After tea there are lots of games to play. It is Nellie's turn to pin the tail on the pig.

Prizegiving

Ned wins first prize for the best fancy dress. All the other monsters win prizes as well.

Going Home

The party is over. Mum Lamb gives Nellie and Ned a
bag of little presents to take home.

First published in 1986
Usborne Publishing Ltd
20 Garrick St, London
WC2 9BJ, England
© Usborne Publishing Ltd 1986

The name of Usborne and the
device 🐝 are Trade Marks of
Usborne Publishing Ltd.

Printed in Portugal